The
Thief of Colours

REED

Ben Brown & Helen Taylor

It had been a dreary day — murky, damp and dull — down in the swamp where Pukeko lived with her young.

'What a gloomy place this is,' she thought. 'My chicks need something bright, something happy, something colourful to look at. Where will I get it?' she wondered.

As night closed in and the gloom got gloomier, Pukeko snuggled down warm in her nest, thinking, 'Red like the sunrise, blue like the sky …' And so she slept, dreaming of colours.

The next day, even while the stars were still shining, Pukeko set off towards the very edge of the slowly disappearing night. Once there she settled down to wait by a kowhai tree. Sunrise would be soon. Another day was about to begin.

The sun, being by far the most important thing in the sky, liked to surround itself in bold and swirling red — the colour of most important things. So every sunrise is announced by dancing flashes of fire and a glorious blaze of every kind of red imaginable.

This morning was no different. There was the glorious blaze of red and the dancing flashes of fire. And there in the middle was the sun, so full of the importance of its own rising that it didn't see Pukeko reaching out and stealing some of the colour of its glory.

And then, because it was there, she also took yellow from the kowhai tree.
'After all,' she thought, 'red and yellow go so well together.'

B ut a dancing flash of fire had seen what Pukeko was up to. And Tui, in his kowhai tree, was not impressed at all.
'Hey!' he clanged, as tui do. 'Give me back my yellow!'
And he took off after Pukeko in a flurry of clangs and flapping wings.

The dancing flash of fire followed, spitting sparks from the morning sky. Sun, now over the importance of its own rising, bellowed from above, 'Pukeko — give me back my red!'

But Pukeko would not give up the colours.

The dancing flash of fire spat sparks that singed Pukeko's backside. And Tui clanged so loudly that Pukeko could hardly think which way to run. So she ran anywhere and everywhere through forest and scrub.

She ran until at last the dancing flash had run out of sparks and Tui thought he'd probably clanged enough, and anyway he had a kowhai tree to keep an eye on.

So Pukeko escaped with the red and yellow.

Above her the sun got on with its job of warming and lighting the world, and because of all the morning's excitement, everything seemed suddenly brighter. Even the sky looked bluer today.
'Beautifully blue,' thought Pukeko.
'I must have some of that!'

The sky was wearing a wonderful cloak of different blues, and threads of blue from his cloak had caught on the tops of the highest mountains, waiting for Wind to free them and take them back from where they'd come.

Pukeko quickly flew to the top of the mountains and grabbed a thread that was caught there. But Wind saw her and quickly gave chase.
'That's not your thread,' he howled angrily.
'That's what you think!' thought Pukeko, and she started to fly for home as quickly as her wings would carry her.

But she wasn't fast enough.

In the flap of a wing, Wind caught up with Pukeko and tangled her in the stolen thread. It was as though Pukeko had suddenly forgotten how to fly as she came tumbling out of the sky.

But she refused to let go of the thread.

Down, down, down she fell.

'Let go!' screamed the wind. 'Let go or you'll crash!'

As the ground got closer and closer, even Pukeko saw that this was true. She let go of the thread and Wind quickly untangled her. Pukeko flapped her wings like she had never flapped before.

The tops of the trees rushed by as she frantically tried to slow herself, flapping for all she was worth. Down she fell, through the forest tops, the feathered ferns, the flax, and finally with a not-so-gentle THUNK! she landed on the forest floor.

And even though she'd lost the thread, she still had some of the blue that made it beautiful.

So once again Pukeko set off for home, closely guarding her precious colours.

All at once she heard a raucous, clamouring call.

'Green, green, look at my green! Isn't it wonderful?! Isn't it green?!' shrieked an amazingly coloured bird.

'Wonderful indeed,' thought Pukeko. 'I must have some of that!'

The bird was so full of its own song that it didn't see Pukeko creep up from behind and help herself to a tail feather.

But a group of other green birds, waiting their turn to sing, had seen what she'd done.

'H ey!' squawked one.
'You!' shrieked another.
'Thief, thief, thief,' yelled three or four more.
Louder and louder and angrier and angrier,
the green birds surrounded Pukeko, jostling
and pushing.

The squawking got even louder and the
pushing got rougher, and soon the green
birds began fighting each other, beaks
flashing and feathers flying.

To Pukeko's great surprise the green birds
soon forgot all about her so she quietly
slipped away in all the confusion.

ukeko was almost home when, suddenly and silently, a great white kotuku swept gracefully overhead. As the heron flew, even the air around it seemed to glow.

'Oh yes, yes, yes!' thought Pukeko. 'I must have some of that!'

And she set off after Kotuku.

But it had been a long day and Pukeko was very tired. Her wings were never going to be a match for the heron's. Soon she knew that she would have to land or she would fall out of the sky again.

Turning for home she was soon over her swamp where she landed with all her hard-won colours but without the beautiful white she had tried to take from the heron. Then, just as she was settling back in her nest, a flash of pure light caught her eye and a shining white feather floated down towards her. All the other colours glowed in welcome.

As the sun set slowly with its fiery reds, Pukeko thought about rainbows and wondered where she could find one in the morning.